# OVER the RIVER
## A Turkey's Tale

# Over the River

by Lydia Maria Child

# OVER *the* RIVER
## A Turkey's Tale

**Derek Anderson**

based on the song by Lydia Maria Child

### SCHOLASTIC INC.

New York  Toronto  London  Auckland  Sydney

Mexico City  New Delhi  Hong Kong  Buenos Aires

for Alyssa—D. A.

ISBN-13: 978-0-439-90061-4
ISBN-10: 0-439-90061-1

Text copyright © 2005 by Simon & Schuster, Inc.
Illustrations copyright © 2005 by Derek Anderson. All rights reserved.
Published by Scholastic Inc., 557 Broadway, New York, NY 10012,
by arrangement with Simon & Schuster Books for Young Readers,
Simon & Schuster Children's Publishing Division. SCHOLASTIC and
associated logos are trademarks and/or registered trademarks
of Scholastic Inc.

12 11 10 9 8 7 6 5 4 3 2 1                    6 7 8 9 10 11/0

Printed in the U.S.A.                                   40

First Scholastic printing, October 2006
Book design by Daniel Roode
The text for this book is set in Fontoon.
The illustrations for this book are rendered in acrylic paint.

OVER THE RIVER AND THROUGH THE WOODS by Donald White
Copyright © 1988 by Shawnee Press, Inc. (ASCAP)
International copyright secured. All rights reserved.
Reprinted by permission.

Based on the song "Over the River and
Through the Woods" by Lydia
Maria Child.

Over the river and through the woods,

to Grandmother's house we go.

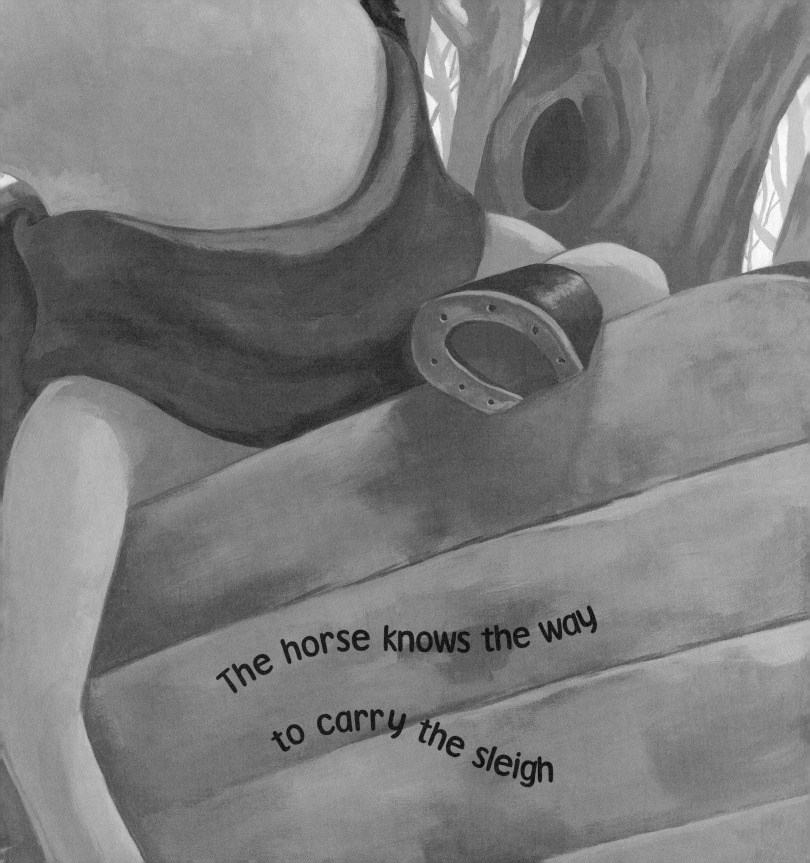

The horse knows the way
to carry the sleigh

through white and drifted snow.

Over the river and through the woods,

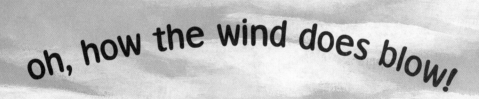
oh, how the wind does blow!

It stings the toes and bites the nose,

as over the ground we go.

Over the river and through the woods,

to have a first-rate play.

Oh,
hear
the
bell
RING,

ting-
a-
ling-
ling,

hurrah for Thanksgiving Day!

Over the river and through the woods,

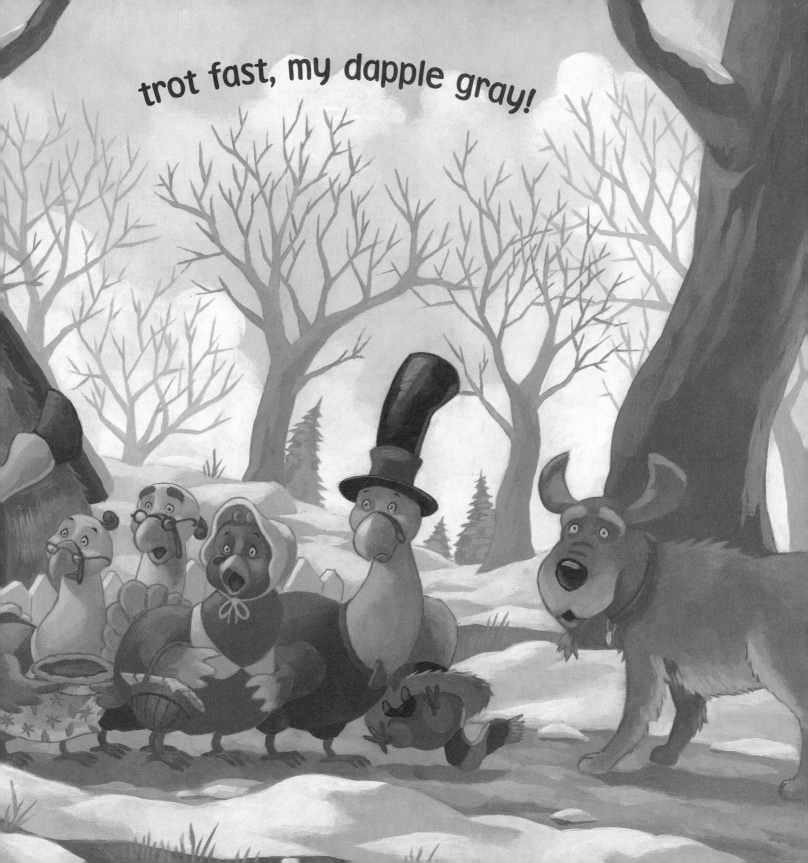

spring over the ground

like a hunting hound,

for this is Thanksgiving Day.

# Over the River

## by Lydia Maria Child